Water Rat's Picnic

by Alison Uttley

Pictures by Margaret Tempest

COLLINS COLOUR CUBS

One day Water-rat came out of his house by the river-side and strolled down his garden path. He picked a sprig of flowering rush and fastened it in his buttonhole. Then he whistled a sea-shanty and went towards his boat-house.

There lay the neatest, prettiest little boat you ever saw! She had a pair of slender oars. She was made of polished elm and her name, the *Saucy Nancy*, was picked out in gold letters. A couple of cushions lay on the seat, and a water-jar was in the bow.

Water-rat was very proud of his boat.

On this particular fine day Water-rat took a duster from his pocket and whisked the specks from the boat. He took the stone jar to the spring and filled it with clear water. He polished his copper kettle and packed the picnic basket.

"Where might you be going today, Sir?" asked Mrs Webster, his house-keeper.

"I'm going to see some young friends of mine," said Water-rat. "I shall try to persuade them to join me in a water picnic. They've never seen a boat, I believe."

"Then they'll have a surprise when they see the *Saucy Nancy*," said Mrs Webster.

Water-rat settled himself in the boat and paddled peacefully upstream.

Green dragonflies darted here and there, and a kingfisher shot by like a blue arrow. Among the reeds at the water's edge a brown water-hen was busy with a heap of washing.

"A good drying day," said Water-rat, and the water-hen looked up from her work.

"The ducks are very tiresome," she said. "They tease me and carry off the washing, and I have no peace."

"Never mind, you've got a fine young family to help you," said Water-rat.

"Fourteen children," said the water-hen proudly, "and every one a champion swimmer."

Water-rat took up the oars and rowed some distance. Hare hailed him from the bank. Then he moored the boat to the roots of a willow and leaped out. He walked across the fields to Grey Rabbit's house, and he tapped at the door.

"Come in! Come in!" called Grey Rabbit, who was busy making strawberry jam.

"Oh! Water-rat! How pleased I am to see you!" she cried. "Do sit down and rest. I shan't be long now. The strawberries are bubbling."

"Nice smell," said Water-rat, sinking into the rocking-chair, and wiping his forehead. "We have no strawberries by the river."

"What kind of jam do you make?" asked Grey Rabbit.

"Lily-bud jam," said Water-rat. "Mrs Webster makes it from the lilies in our backwater."

Grey Rabbit ladled the jam into a row of little glass jars. She covered each with a strawberry leaf and tied it with a blade of grass.

"That's finished!" She sat down and fanned her hot face.

"I came to invite you and Squirrel to go for a picnic," said Water-rat. "My boat is moored by the old willow and the food is aboard."

"A picnic! A boat!" cried Grey Rabbit, clapping her hands.

"A boat? A real live boat?" called Squirrel, dancing in.

"A picnic? A real live picnic?" shouted Hare, popping his head in at the window.

"I'm afraid my boat will only hold three," said Water-rat coldly.

Hare came into the room. "Look here," he cried. "Do you mean to say you are going on a picnic without me? It's impossible!"

He sank, half-fainting, on a chair. Squirrel loosened his collar and Grey Rabbit fetched a glass of primrose wine. Hare sipped it with little groans.

"I'm afraid we can't go, Water-rat. We can't leave Hare behind," said Squirrel.

"I have a plan," said Water-rat.

"Yes? What is it?" they asked, and Hare opened his eyes and forgot to faint.

"Surely you could run faster than the *Saucy Nancy*, Hare? Suppose you race along the river-bank, while I row Grey Rabbit and Squirrel. Then you can choose the place for the picnic and we will all have a feast under the trees."

"That's a good idea," said Hare. "It isn't the boat I want, but the picnic."

Hare and Squirrel went upstairs to get ready, and Grey Rabbit followed them.

"I shall wear my goloshes, because it might be wet on the river," said Grey Rabbit.

"I shall take my fishing net," said Hare.

"I shall wear my yellow dress and have my new sunshade," said Squirrel.

They shut the windows and locked the door, and put the key under the mat.

They tripped along by Water-rat's side, asking questions about the boat.

Grey Rabbit carried a pot of strawberry jam, Hare his fishing-net, and Squirrel the pretty little sunshade.

"Oh! How beautiful!" cried Grey Rabbit, when she saw the *Saucy Nancy* under the willow branches.

"You shall steer, Grey Rabbit," said Water-rat, "and Squirrel shall sit on a cushion."

He helped them both into the boat and untied the rope.

"Look at the waves, and the darting fishes, and the green weeds!" cried Grey Rabbit. She jumped with excitement as she saw the water so near.

"Good-bye. Good-bye," called Hare. "I shall meet you soon. Take care of the food and don't fall in the river."

He galloped along the bank and was soon out of sight.

Squirrel twirled her sunshade, and spread out her tail. She glanced at her reflection in the clear river and dabbled her paw.

"Oh! Oh!" she cried. "A fish has bitten me! Oh! I didn't know fish could bite."

"Yes," warned Water-rat. "They like a dainty morsel."

Squirrel leaned over the side to watch the fish playing hide and seek under the boat's shadow. Grey Rabbit steered past small rocks and islands.

They saw a green frog sitting among the water buttercups with a little fishing rod. They saw the untidy house where the blue kingfisher lived, and the neat cottages of the water-rats. They stopped to chat with the water-hen, and they admired the fourteen little chicks which swam squeaking round the boat.

"Come away, you naughty children," scolded their mother. "Don't go worrying Grey Rabbit and Mister Water-rat."

There was a scurry and a flurry, and a loud quacking as a flock of white ducks came hurrying up.

"Dear me!" cried the water-hen. "Here they are again! Come away children. Come away!"

The ducks swam up to the boat, diving and pushing.

"Where are you landlubbers going?" they asked.

"For a picnic," said Water-rat.

One duck snatched Squirrel's sunshade and carried it off with peals of quacking laughter. Another pulled the strings of Grey Rabbit's apron and swam away with the little blue apron on her shoulders. Another twitched the ribbon from Squirrel's tail, and there was such a commotion, such a rocking of the boat and a splash of water that nobody noticed another duck seize the picnic basket.

"Oh! Oh!" cried Grey Rabbit and Squirrel.

"It's outrageous!" said Water-rat.

He stared at one of the ducks. "Is it possible? Has she taken the picnic basket?"

The duck held the little basket and tried to open it. As she struggled, the basket slipped and went down, down to the bottom of the river.

"I'll get it," muttered Water-rat. He took off his velvet coat and dived overboard. Down to the bed of the river he went, and there he found the basket. He put his arms round it and swam back to the boat.

Then he clambered over the side, sat upon the basket and rowed away fast.

"Lucky it's lined with mackintosh," said Water-rat. "But I'm sorry about your apron, Grey Rabbit, and sunshade, Squirrel."

"I'll make another apron," said Grey Rabbit.

"And will you pick me one of those big, round leaves for a sunshade, Water-rat?" said Squirrel.

Water-rat picked the lily leaf and Squirrel held it over her head.

"Where's Hare?" asked Water-rat, staring at the river bank. "He ought to be somewhere waiting for us."

"Coo-oo," called Grey Rabbit.

"Coo-oo," came a faint reply. Water-rat pulled the boat to the shore and from out of the reeds peered Hare, his coat torn and his net broken.

"Oh dear!" he cried. "I've been chased by a dog, pestered by rabbits and bitten by gnats. And you've been rowing peacefully up the river."

"Not so peacefully," laughed Grey Rabbit. "I've lost my blue apron, Hare."

"And I've lost my sunshade," added Squirrel.

"And we nearly lost the picnic basket," said Water-rat.

"That would have been a calamity," muttered Hare.

He took the basket from Water-rat. Then he sat down under a tree to nurse it. Now and then he peeped through the meshes, or tried to unfasten the catch, but the basket was tightly shut.

Grey Rabbit and Squirrel ran about, picking up sticks, and Water-rat carried the kettle and water-jar to the hollow by the trees.

They heaped up the sticks and made a big fire.

"Come along, Hare. You have more breath than any of us. You can be the blow-bellows," said Squirrel, as she balanced the kettle on top.

Hare puffed out his cheeks and blew hard. Soon the kettle began to sing in its high shrill voice.

Water-rat unfastened the picnic basket and spread out the dainties.

Hare leaped for joy when he saw the patties and sandwiches and jellies in their waterproof wrappers.

What a feast there was! They laughed and sang and told their adventures, and quite forgot their troubles. Hare was very hungry, for, he explained, he had run for miles while they had been resting in the boat.

They took the cups to the river edge and washed them and dried them on the grasses. They repacked the basket, then they sat down to watch the river whirling below them.

Hare crept softly away and climbed into the boat. He untied the rope and pushed her into the stream.

"You didn't know I could row," he called. "It's quite easy."

"Oh Hare! Take care!" shrieked Squirrel.

"Sit down, Hare," said Water-rat. "You'll upset her if you stand up."

Hare sat down with a thump and the boat shook. He dipped the oars deep in the river and dragged up some weeds. Then the oars waved wildly, Hare's feet flew up, and he shot backwards into the water.

"Save me! Save me! I'm drowning!" he cried, kicking and struggling.

Out of the shadows came the company of ducks, one with the blue apron over her shoulders, another with the red sunshade above her head, and another with a ribbon round her neck.

They circled round Hare and grabbed him by his fur. One took his left ear and another his right, another his leg and the fourth his coat tail. Then they swam to the shore with him.

They pushed him on the bank and away they went, cackling with laughter.

Squirrel and Grey Rabbit dried him with their handkerchiefs. Poor Hare crouched over the fire, shivering.

"It's very wet in the river," he said. "I never knew that boat wasn't safe."

"You will have to run all the way home," said Grey Rabbit. "It will keep you from catching cold."

Water-rat swam after the little boat and the pair of oars. He rowed back, dried the boat and wiped the cushions.

"I told you," said Hare, sternly. "That boat isn't safe."

"What you want is a paddle-steamer," grunted Water-rat.

"Yes," agreed Hare. "That's what I want. I'm going home! I feel a chill in my bones."

The others seated themselves in the boat, and Water-rat turned to Grey Rabbit.

"Would you like to see my house?" he asked. "Mrs Webster, my housekeeper, will be pleased to welcome you.

"There's watercress growing in my stream, and I'll give you some to take home."

Grey Rabbit and Squirrel were delighted, and Water-rat turned the boat up the stream and stopped at the boathouse at the bottom of his garden.

Then they walked up the garden path and entered the damp little house.

On a table in the hall stood an aquarium with duck-weed and sticklebacks and minnows.

Squirrel could hardly tear herself away from this watery scene, but Water-rat led the way to the parlour. It was very wet, and Grey Rabbit was glad she had her goloshes. Squirrel tucked her feet high as she sat on the bulrush chair.

"Mrs Webster, will you bring some of your water-lily jam for my guests?" asked Water-rat.

Mrs Webster fetched the little pots of lily jam and packed them in a bag for Grey Rabbit to carry.

"I'll get the watercress," said Water-rat, and he hurried away.

"Oh, Miss Grey Rabbit and Miss Squirrel!" said Mrs Webster. "I am glad to see you. And how is Mister Hare? I suppose he couldn't go to the picnic, being too big for the boat?"

"Oh dear!" cried Grey Rabbit. "I'd forgotten about him! He fell in the river, Mrs Webster. We must hurry home."

Water-rat came back with the watercress in a basket.

"We must go home," said Grey Rabbit, as she thanked him. "Poor Hare is waiting for us, all wet."

"Good-bye Mrs Webster," they called, as they hurried away. Water-rat rowed swiftly, and soon they were back at the old willow tree.

"Thank you dear Water-rat. Thank you," they said, and they scampered home as fast as they could.

"Hare! Hare!" they called as they went into the house. "Guess what we did! We went to Water-rat's house and we saw a goldfish and – Hare, where are you?"

A violent sneeze shook the house.

They ran upstairs. There was Hare in bed with his head in a blanket.

"A-tishoo!" sneezed Hare. "I thought you were both drowned. Make me some elder-flower tea, Grey Rabbit, A-tishoo!"

Squirrel and Grey Rabbit raced around with herbs and hot water and soon Hare was snug with his teapot of elder-flower tea by his side.

"Now, tell me all about it," said he.

So little Grey Rabbit began to tell of Mrs Webster and the aquarium. Hare shut his eyes, and before she had finished he was fast asleep.

She tiptoed downstairs and joined Squirrel who was resting by the fire.

Pit-pat! Pit-pat! Little footsteps came flipping to the door. There was muffled laughter and a shuffle and a flop.

Squirrel and Grey Rabbit looked at each other.

"Who can it be?" they whispered.

Pit-pat! Little footsteps went flipping down the garden path.

Grey Rabbit opened the door a crack. On the doorstep lay her blue apron, rather torn, and very wet.

"Oh how glad I am to get my little apron again," she cried, and she hung it by the fire to dry.

But the sunshade never came back. The ducks liked it so much they wouldn't part with it. Any day you could see them swimming down the river, one of them carrying Squirrel's sunshade, and another playing with Squirrel's ribbon bow.

Alison Uttley's original story has been
abridged for this book.

ISBN 0 00 194182 8